Beulah & Blanche

&

The Bubblegum Ranch

Hi Brittan
'A merry heart is good medicine'
it says in Proverbs. Hope you
enjoy these silly poems your old
art teacher did. Glad you are
doing so well.

Best Wishes

Annette Proctor

Beulah & Blanche
&
The Bubblegum Ranch

the

art

&

poems

of

Aunty Nett

Manufactured in the United States of America

ISBN-13: 978-1494343491
ISBN-10: 1494343495

Cover Art and Interior Illustration by Annette Proctor

First Edition December 2013

To my adult children, who patiently endured all my poetry readings and rereadings while I worked out the kinks and a special word of thanks to my son who diligently found and collected them all with their illustrations and compiled them into this very book.

Beulah and Blanche and the Bubblegum Ranch

Down near the town
Of Chewersville Branch
Beulah and Blanche have
A bubble gum ranch.

Hundreds of acres
Of bubble gum trees
With every flavor
That could ever please.

You've got to be careful with bubble gum trees,
And pick when the time is just right;
For if you wait just a day too long
You're in for a terrible sight.

The girls look closely, and sniff
With a keen sense of smell,
If the gum is too ripe and begins to soften
The fruit will certainly swell.

A beautiful sight,
   Or so I've been told,
But none of that gum
   Could ever be sold.

If they wait, just a day too long,
   The trees will burp and bubble,
Then the girls will certainly have
   Some extremely bad, gum trouble.

First smaller, then bigger
   The tree bubbles grow,
A very strange sight,
   Wouldn't you know.

Smaller, bigger, POP!
   Then SPLAT!
Sticky, gooey gum
   On your hands, shoes and lap.

Everyone runs to get away
   From that place;
As they pull soft, warm gum
   From their hair, neck and face.

Use your imagination
    Can't you just see,
Row after row of
    Bubble gum trees.

Row after row
    Pink bubbles abound,
Soft and pink
    Long and or round.

If the trees blow the bubbles,
    The trees have the fun.
The trees blow the bubbles,
    And the kids get none.

But don't you worry children,
    Don't you whine,
The girls know just when to pick,
    They know the perfect time.

Lavinnia

Lavinnia was skinny-ah,
she never could gain weight,
people who have known her
say she ate and ate and ate.

You could always find her
eating cookies, pies and cakes.
For breakfast she'd have donuts,
and five bowls of sugared flakes.

Brunch was often cinnamon rolls
with bananas and some chips,
and if that wouldn't satisfy,
to the chips she'd add some dip.

At noon, Lavinnia was heard to mumble,
"This is the time my stomach will rumble.
I'm starving! Why is lunch so late?
I don't see any food, I don't see a plate."

Lunch was something to behold,
hamburger, fries and a drink that's cold;
salad and a bowl of soup,
vanilla ice cream topped with chocolate goop.

Right after school, just about three,
Lavinnia rushed home, but not just for tea.
"What's for snack?" Lavinnia would call,
"How about an apple, milk and a popcorn ball."

Followed by crackers topped with cheese,
and a bowl of yogurt if you please.
A dozen cookies on a plate,
a handful of raisins and a few dates.

Mother had dinner on the table by five;
ham, baked potato, sour cream and chives,
a salad, a vegetable, a hot buttered roll,
a glass of chocolate milk and pudding in a bowl.

Just before bed, around about nine,
Lavinnia had her bed-snack time.
"Nothing too heavy," Lavinnia would say,
"A nice coke float, brought in on a tray."

Lavinnia was skinny, ah until one day,
she got on the scale to see what she'd weigh.
Mercy me! Lo and behold,
that old scale had a tale to be told.

Lavinnia then had to sit right down,
Lavinnia had gained three hundred pounds.

Milt Wore a Kilt

Milt wore a kilt,
he liked to a lot.
Milt wore a kilt
though he wasn't a Scot.

Milt wore plaids,
though he wasn't a Scot.
He went to the shop
and that's what he bought.

Milt told stories
of wars that he'd fought,
battles in the Highlands,
and the enemies he'd caught.

Milt told stories,
of how he'd been shot;
stories of bravery
and wounds that he got.

Milt talked with a brogue,
just like a Scot.
It sounded like his tongue
was tied up in a knot.

Milt saw himself as a legend,
a true heroic Scot,
with many twists and turns
in each and every plot.

Milt loved scotch broth
cooked in an iron pot,
with lots of lamb and barley,
served really piping hot.

A 'bonnie lass' is what
Milt really sought.
He'd play her the bagpipes,
(he was of course, self-taught.)

Why did Milt
want to be a Scot?
He was Chinese!
A Scot he was not!

He changed his name
to Milton Mac Shmott,
his knees were cold
and he shivered a lot.

His stories were fibs
in which he was caught.
But still he insisted,
"I am—and will stay a full-blooded Scot!"

Where did Milt live
dressed as a Scot?
He lived in Alaska,
where Scots, there are naught.

Oh Say Can You Sneeze

Have you ever wondered at the words people sneeze?
How varied and curious are the sounds of these.

The man next door was short and light,
He had a bald head and rode an old bike.

His sneezes registered on the Richter Scale;
Causing pictures to fall and old folks to pale.

"Oh-Wha-Who!" he sneezed for all to hear,
And the clouds would part, the skies would clear.

A cousin of mine, who came from the coast,
Had a sneeze unusual of which he would boast.

"McTavish!" he roared with a certain resound,
As we scattered for shelter hastily found.

"Ah-hersheee!" We called the candy bar sneeze.
My own dear father was the creator of these.

He'd fling his arms and kick his left leg,
And always seemed pleased with the sound that he'd made.

The giggles sneeze was perfected by an aunt,
With a high pitched voice that could shrivel a plant.

"Tee-hee-hee!" She blew in her lady-like way,
God bless you, someone, somewhere would say.

Duane

Duane's game brought him great fame.
He carried the flame to the interstate game.

Duane's brother, whose name was Blaine,
  also played at Duane's game.
But Blaine's skills were unfortunately lame;
  his efforts tame.

Duane's mother was a titled dame;
this too brought Duane considerable fame.

Sadly the day came, when Duane was off his game.
The shame came due to his aim.

His reputation was never the same.
He had only himself to blame.

Duane's Brother Blaine

Blaine didn't use to use a cane;
but he'd been stupid and not used his brain.

Blaine loved to skip in the rain,
while walking his dog, who was a Great Dane.

Blaine's Dane saw a cat walking in the rain.
This drove the Dane to go joyfully insane.

The results caused Blaine considerable pain;
and that's why Blaine now uses a cane.

Oh Groan

Oh groan, here comes Joan.

On and on she'll drone,
when on the phone,
no wonder she's alone.

She has this tone,
kind of a moan,
when she asks for a loan.

Poor Joan, she's all alone,
eating a cone,
which she's dribbled on her dress she has sewn.

Never mind,
she's in the zone,
eating her cone,
skinny as a bone.

I'll be glad when she's grown.

Raoul McSweeney

Did you know that cat
      Named Raoul McSweeney?
He ate very little for his tummy was teeney.

A little fish
      A little cream,
Was all he needed
      Or so it did seem.

His appetite was small
      But still he grew,
A large MEOW
      From a tiny mee-ewe.

Little feet
      Into bigger paws,
Lovely long tail
      And very sharp claws.

How did Raoul
      Get to be so big?
When he nibbled so little,
      And never ate like a pig?

I'll tell you the truth,
      The secret I found
When I decided to follow
      McSweeney around.

That sneaky McSweeny
      Was eating midnight snacks,
Cheese and a mouse sandwich
      Packed in his lunch sack.

And during the day
      When no one was around,
In between meals
      He ate bugs he had found.

Clever and Smart Like Me

Four raccoons are in
my own plum tree,
they're eating plums
and laughing at me.

Their little masked faces
are cute for sure;
with their black striped tails
and long gray fur.

The way they were eating,
the plums would be gone.
I had to do something,
and didn't have very long.

I hollered up into
that old plum tree.
"Quit eating my plums!"
"Quit laughing at me!"

That didn't help,
it didn't help at all.
They laughed so hard
I thought they'd fall.

The raccoons, like acrobats,
flying around the tree.
They picked up some plums
and threw them at me.

That's enough!
They'd crossed over the line.
Those plums weren't theirs,
in fact they were mine.

I had been patient,
but now I was sore.
If that's what they wanted,
this would be war!

I needed a plan,
to spoil their game.
If you'd been there,
you'd feel the same.

Please don't think
I'm mean in the least,
just want them to find
someplace else for their feast.

I threw water balloons
and Frisbees I had;
they dodged all of them,
cause my aim was so bad.

A large barking dog
at the foot of the tree,
was laughed at too, just like
they'd laughed at me.

Water from the hose
they thought great fun.
I'm out of ideas.
The raccoons may have won.

Suddenly an idea popped
into my head;
Those raccoons were hungry,
They needed to be fed.

I've been going at this
In all the wrong way.
I thought of a plan that
should work out okay.

I brought them a lot
of bubble gum to chew.
They stopped eating plums
and pink bubbles they blew.

I brought them some taffy
saying, "Come take a peek."
That kept them all chewing,
till the middle of next week.

In order to save
all the plums on your tree,
You must be clever
and smart like me.

Don't holler or throw things
to save each plum.
Just offer them candy
and plenty of gum.

Kevin Claude Van Dipplenodd

Kevin Claude Van Dipplenodd,
was fearless and brave as could be;
Except for the time he was stung on his toe
by quite a large bumble-type-bee.

Kevin Claude Van Dipplenodd
was fearless and brave as could be;
except for the time he was chased by a mouse
and he cried for two days, maybe three.

Kevin Claude Van Dipplenodd
was fearless and brave as could be;
except for the time a butterfly flew,
on his shoulder and then on his knee.

Kevin Claude Van Dipplenodd
was fearless and brave as could be;
except for the time his mother served soup,
and called it, her special split pea.

Kevin Claude Van Dipplenodd
was fearless and brave as could be;
except for the time he played in the sand
and was pinched by a crab from the sea.

Kevin Claude Van Dipplenodd
was fearless and brave as could be;
except for the time his zipper got stuck
and he simply could not get it free.

Kevin Claude Van Dipplenodd
was fearless and brave as could be;
except for the time he played with his dog
and got bit by more than one flea.

Kevin Claude Van Dipplenodd
was fearless and brave as could be;
except for the time he played at the shore
and his castle was washed out to sea.

Kevin Claude Van Dipplenodd
was fearless and brave as could be;
except for the time he ran after the ball
and ran into the old willow tree.

Kevin Claude Van Dipplenodd
was fearless and brave as could be;
except for most of the time, or all of the time;
after all he's only just three.

Linda Lou and the Lost Shoe

A little lady lizard by the name of Linda Lou,
sat on a rock sobbing, oh boohoo, boohoo, boohoo.
"For why are you crying?" asked her friend Cindy Sue.
"For because, I lost my new high heeled shoe,"
cried little Linda Lou.
"It matched a hat and dress,
that are a beautiful hue of blue."

"Not to worry!" shouted her friend Cindy Sue,
"We'll just form a crew,
to find your lost shoe that's blue."

At first her crew was few, just about two,
but then it grew and grew to more than just a few,
led by a lizard named Hugh.
"Thank you," sobbed little Linda Lou,
"I was going to a party with some friends from the zoo."
Hugh and the lizard crew searched long and hard
for the lost new, blue shoe.
They could tell the little lady lizard
was in an awful stew.
Then one of the crew knew he'd found a clue,
and he knew just what to do.
That clue drew the crew
to a tiny-girl shrew from a place called Peru.
An interview of the shrew,
pursued by the crew,
led by Hugh, solved the lost-blue-shoe-issue.
The shrew gave up the shoe to the crew
and departed down a stream in a tiny leaf canoe.
The crew and Hugh celebrated the return of the shoe
with a root beer brew and some pretzels to chew.
Cindy Sue had to issue a tissue
to little Linda Lou for her tears of joy,
boohoo, boohoo, boohoo.

Snyder

Snyder, a spider, was bored with his web.
"I want more room and need a new bed."

His web though plain was still fairly big,
it stretched from a bush over to a twig.

Snyder wasn't satisfied, he wanted fancier too,
"I'll learn to knit, that's what I'll do!"

He knitted a guest room then crocheted a bed;
he knitted curtains and died them bright red.

Snyder worked long with no time for rest,
he added a dining room with a view to the west.

He learned to make lace in addition to his skills;
then made some cushions with ruffles and frills.

More and more rooms were beautifully spun,
until at last Snyder said, "I guess that I'm done."

Snyder's web was a work of great art,
"It's too fine to live in, I'll have to depart."

And so sad but proud Snyder moved out,
from the world's finest web, without a doubt.

He spun himself a traditional condo web,
"Two car garage and patio is enough," he said.

But while sleeping and dreaming new plans in his head,
kept stirring and turning though asleep in his bed.

The very next morning Snyder decided to 'add-on'
and he's still remodeling long after his first home was gone.

That's why you see so many webs in your yard.
Snyder's a builder and he loves working hard.

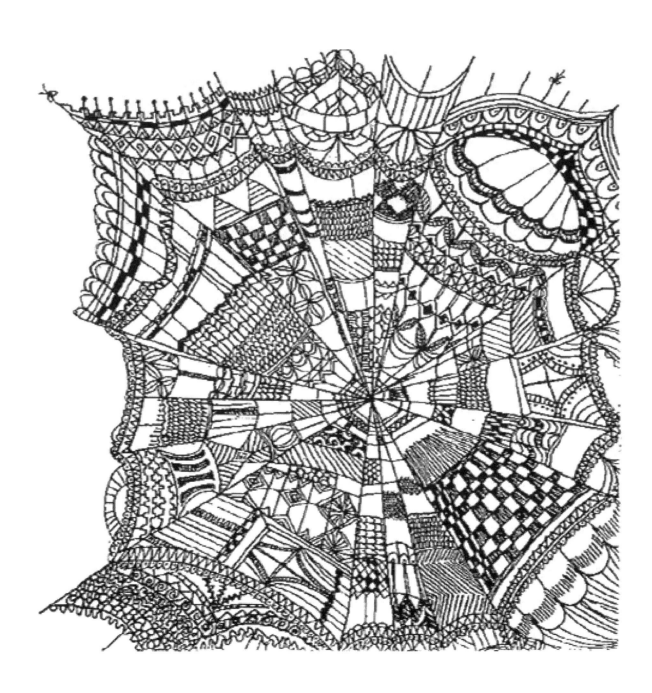

Eleanor

Eleanor spun a very fine web,
it was the best in the yard
all the spiders had said.

Kind of like lace or macramé,
but still very strong,
and that's what they'd say.

But one of the spiders, Snyder by name,
was jealous of Eleanor
and all her great fame.

Snyder bragged *his* web was certainly the best,
his was stronger
and prettier than *all* of the rest.

He didn't do just fancy designs,
No! He did portraits
within his web lines.

The mayor of spiderville had a deep thought.
I'm calling for a vote,
right here on this web spot.

All the spiders gathered around,
some from the air
and some up from the ground.

The end of this story is sad but true,
several flies were seen texting
and into the webs they flew.

I don't have to tell you what was in each spider's head.
I don't have to tell you
what happens to texting flies when they land on a web.

The Junk Food Caterpillar

Everyone knows just how moms feel
about eating the food she has for a meal.

Everyone's mom says, "Eat your greens,
grow up strong and get your plate clean."

Everyone's mom says, "Don't eat junk,
your body won't grow and your brain might flunk."

Even a caterpillar I once knew
was told by his mom just what to do.

But he didn't listen, he didn't care;
he wanted cotton candy like you get at the fair.

He liked snow cones, candy bars and cokes;
didn't want spinach, lettuce or artichokes.

He'd often say while eating some candy,
"Eat what I eat and life will be dandy."

"YOU ARE WHAT YOU EAT is just an old adage;
when I get old I'll eat string beans and cabbage."

"Just give me all the chocolate I can hold,
don't give me lectures and please don't scold."

So off he went with a big happy grin,
not knowing the terrible shape he was in.

One day he looked up from his place on the ground
and saw other caterpillars had wings and were flying around.

He was astonished and surprised as he gasped,
"How did that happen?" he finally asked.

They were his friends so they fluttered down low,
"Why we're butterflies now, didn't you know?"

"You should've eaten your salads, with all the right things,
your body needs vitamins to grow these fine wings."

He cried, "What can I do, is it too late?
Can I still grow strong if I clean my plate?"

"Your growth is slow that's for sure,
but eating good foods will be the cure."

With that the butterflies flew high in the air,
and the caterpillar started eating some spinach near there.

Fred, Ned and Ted versus John, Ron and Shawn

Fred, Ned and Ted
never could get ahead.
That's because they always slept in,
and hardly ever got out of bed.

John, Ron and Shawn
were long gone for work by dawn.
They were great friends
and almost always got a long.

Fred, Ned and Ted
fought a lot, people said.
They didn't like to work,
work is what they'd dread.

John, Ron and Shawn
often broke out in song.
They'd come together and sing
out on their very own lawn.

Fred, Ned and Ted
asked others for drinks and bread.
They'd sniff and cry and pretend
that soon they might even be dead.

John, Ron and Shawn knew
Fred, Ned and Ted were cons.
That they were just plain lazy;
And that was just plain wrong.

Fred, Ned and Ted
didn't care what anyone said;
as long as they were fed,
then would go back to bed.

Listen to what I have said
about Fred, Ned and Ted;
"Get up out of bed;
earn your own stinking bread!"

Listen to John, Ron and Shawn
who work and get along.
They are very happy,
cheering folks with their song.

A Frog?

"There's a frog in my throat,"
        that's what mom said,
he must have crawled in
        while I slept in my bed.

Now's the problem,
        what to do?
Will he come on out
        if I call "You-who?"

Maybe if I hang a fly
        on the end of my nose,
he'll come out quickly.
        Look! There he goes.

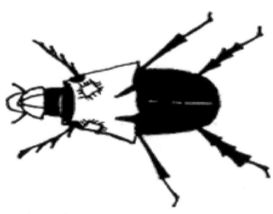

A Beetle Named Bob

A beetle named Bob was looking for work,
he was tired and hungry and needed a new shirt.

Down on his luck, sad and forlorn;
wondering about life and why he was born.

Depressed and gloomy as he climbed through the trash,
he needed some money, he needed some cash.

His uncle Nolan, a dung beetle by trade,
had done quite well, a lot of money he'd made.

But Bob just wasn't called to blue collar work,
he fancied himself an intellect so the dung he did shirk.

Dave Lives in a Cave

Dave's expression is grave.
    He lives in a cave.

Rarely does he shave,
    too dark in his cave.

Company he'd crave
    but few are brave
        to visit Dave in his cave.

You may hear Dave rant and rave
    at the entrance to his cave.

I just keep walking,
    smile and wave,
        until Dave learns to behave.

A Collie Named Molly

A collie named Molly
watches over a
three year old named Holly.

Molly keeps Holly
from play that is
foolish or folly

Holly's favorite toy
is a dolly
she named Polly.

Holly took her dolly
for a ride on a trolley,
but the driver known as Wally
said Mollie couldn't go.

Molly was sorry that Wally
wouldn't let her ride on the trolley;
it made her sad and melancholy.

So Molly decided to run to
where the trolley would drop Holly
and her dolly, Polly.

Holly was so happy and jolly
to see Molly
when she got off of that trolley.

They went to eat
their fill of hot tamale,
then they both felt very jolly.

And that's the end, that's the finale.

Huge Hugh

He was really huge,
　　That was huge Hugh.
Hugh was the hugest
I ever knew.

He was so big
　　I thought he'd scrape the sky,
Maybe get in the way
　　Of airplanes that fly by.

His head and shoulders
　　Were above me about a mile,
But I could still see him
　　And his giant smile.

The feet were monstrous
　　They covered acres of ground.
One wrong step
　　And he flatten half our town.

His enormous hands, like great shovels
　　Scooping up clods of dirt,
He'd sit on the ground for hours
　　Making roadways
With only his fingers to do the work.

Often he'd take his lunch
　　When he'd roam,
What he didn't want
　　We could take home.

It took a lot of us
　　To haul it away,
But all that hard work
　　Would really pay.

What that giant
　　Didn't want to eat,
Would feed our village
　　For weeks and weeks.

Of course we were afraid,
　　And stayed out of his way,
But he seemed to be curious,
　　And sort of kind you might say.

Now you can't imagine
        What one day I heard,
His mother calling him,
        I thought—my word!

"Hugh," she said,
        "Hugh come here,
It's time a three year old
        Had his nap, dear."

A giant who still needs a nap,
        It can't be, it really can't!
But then what do I know,
        After all I'm only an ant!

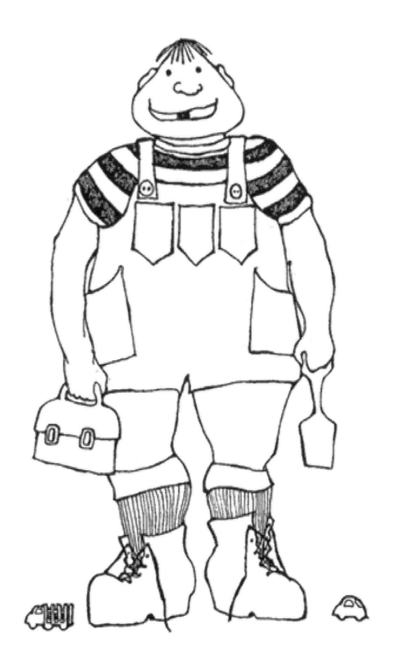

Randolph

Randolph, a dragonfly, was very athletic;
he made all competition look pretty pathetic.

Faster than lightning or horses on a track;
before things got started, he'd gone and come back.

Yes, Randolph was faster than all of the rest;
he had medals to prove it, he wore on his chest.

Backwards, forwards, up and then down,
off to the beach then back into town.

Not only that, that isn't all,
he can pause in the air and not even fall!

Where is he going that requires such speed?
Is there a story here and where will it lead?

Is he a cop in his world of insects and bugs,
catching robbers, bad guys and mean old slugs?

Maybe spying is Randolph's main game,
wearing disguises and changing his name.

He must be a hero, that much is sure;
strong and brave with a heart that is pure.

Curious by nature, I asked all around,
a duck, a rabbit, and an old blood hound.

They said I was crazy and all rolled their eyes,
"Have you not considered Randolph's great size?"

But aren't *you* curious, don't *you* want to know why
Randolph zooms so fast all around in the sky?

The duck shook her tail and bobbled her head,
"You'd better be careful or you're going to be dead!"

"Don't you know," she said, "What he likes to eat?"
"Someone like you," she said, "a very nice treat."

With that, I went quickly right back to my place;
a little more humble but not in disgrace.

I guess I'd better just stay here, where I'm at,
somethings aren't meant to be known by a gnat.

An Odd Kind of Parrot

Uncle Ned Barrett was an odd kind of parrot.

What kind of parrot dines on worms and a carrot?

What kind of parrot has a hat but won't wear it?

What kind of parrot has a pet cat and a ferret?

The kind of parrot that has little or no merit.

The Flatland Four

Horace and Claude
    Hubert and Sam,
Four odd looking ducks
    Who formed their own band.

Horace was tall
    Due to his neck,
His eyes were beady
    And his feathers flecked.

Claude was round,
    Over stuffed you might say;
Big flat feet and eyes
    That rolled in all different ways.

Hubert, he was built low
    To the ground,
Had a body like a sports car
    And a fine rhythm sound.

Sam was the leader
  With a slick-backed feather-do;
Rhinestone jewelry, gold chains,
  And shiny black-patent shoes.

Horace and Claude,
  Hubert and Sam had the
Only rock and roll, funky,
  Square dance band in the land.

They called themselves
  The Flatland Four.
Take a bath, get a date,
  Buy your ticket at the door.

Horace played the geetar,
  Claude the fiddle.
Hubert hit the drums, Sam sang
  Standing in the middle.

None of the group knew
  Much about notes.
But they had lots of rhythm
  And pleased the barnyard folks.

Every Saturday night
  They played at the dance,
All the animals did their own kind of shuffle,
  Did their own kind of prance.

Even bats and mice were seen
  Coming through the door.
No one wanted to miss
  The Flatland Four.

One sad thing I must
  Tell you though,
If you are human
  You can't come to the show.

So if you ever hear them
  On a Saturday night,
Keep right on going, cause—
  You won't get an invite.

Silvia Shannon

Silvia Shannon
Mans the cannon
for the 1812 Overture.

She plays the organ
For Pastor Gordan
    In the church down the road.

She strums the harp
On Sundays in the park,
    It really is quite load.

Her talent's known well,
She has a choir of bells
        That are played for special days.

On Sunday nights
Her fingers take flight
    O'er the piano in wonderful ways.

Tuesday nights
She rides her bike
    To toot her flute in the band.

Thursdays are reserved
For the symphony deserves
    Her skills on the tuba, as only she can.

But Silva's favorite thing to do,
The thing she really looks forward to,
    Is when Silvia Shannon
Mans the cannon
        For the 1812 Overture.

Austin from Boston

Austin from Boston could really run,
The fastest turtle ever, under the sun
You don't believe me? Listen while I tell,
How people exclaim, "What's under that shell?"
Austin moves so fast his shell is a blur;
The only sound heard is a very soft whir.
I know what you're thinking, I know what you'll say;
You think I'm mistaken, only rabbits run that way.
This turtle was special, special indeed.
He lived by a rule, by a personal creed.
Faith moves mountains, and loves impossible feats.
Faith runs races, and makes me very hard to beat.

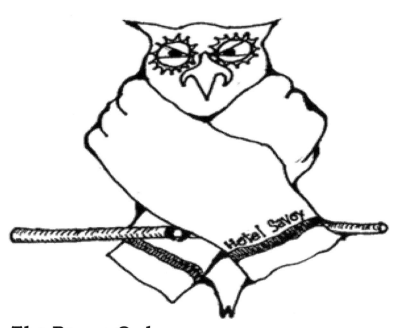

The Brown Owl

There's a brown owl
wrapped in a towel
sitting on a dowel,
listening to a dog howl.
His face wears a scowl,
from hearing that dog howl.
Fowl (in this case an owl) can have a mood
that is foul listening to a dog howl.
He'd rather hear the dog growl
than that incessant howl.
So he flew off to San Paol.

Sir Conrad Kashump

I'd like you to meet Sir Conrad Kashump,
a royal kangaroo of the 'Order of Jump'.

His family goes back a long, long ways,
real blue bloods, born on special days.

Sir Conrad was born a true aristocrat,
he even had a nanny in a little white cap.

All Sir Conrad ever wanted to do,
was jump higher and higher all his life through.

He started by leaping out of nanny's pouch,
which always made nanny a bit of a grouch.

He set jumping records, beating all the rest,
he won plaques, awards and a special vest.

But alas, alack, now he's gone,
his very last jump was far too long.

No one knows just where he landed,
we only know where he last standed.

Who is Neil?

Neil is my friend of great renown,
he's known far and wide,
all over Puget Sound.

He can swim and dive like a real pro,
barking out orders,
putting on a great show.

Talented from the very day he was born,
but you'll never hear Neil
tooting his own horn.

The horns he toots belongs to a friend,
but the melodies are his
from the beginning to the end.

Ha! But can he play ball you may ask.
Pass, bounce or balance it on his nose,
Neil finds them all a very easy task.

In securing the docks Neil has much to say.
During the shows he and his friends
keep the boaters at bay.

His pay seems small for one of such fame,
for one of such renown
in such a competitive game.

Yet Neil is content with only one great desire,
a bucket of food
and a warm dock on which to retire.

A Dress Without Sleeves

A mouse from Belize by the name of Louise
wore dresses without sleeves.
She could feel the breeze
If she didn't wear sleeves.
Her mother said Louise, was very hard to please,
as she'd only eat cheese with a nice spread of fleas
which was hard to get in Belize.

Her brother, Jeeves, loved to tease Louise,
try to make her believe,
yet only deceive his sister Louise.
"You're going to freeze
if you wear dresses without sleeves,
then you'll get a disease,"
teased her brother Jeeves.
"I'd hardly fear to freeze
in the country of Belize," responded Louise.
Jeeves didn't bother Louise,
she just tended to her bees in their hives under the trees
and enjoyed the breeze in her dress without sleeves.

That Strange Deer

I saw this deer, in my rear view mirror;
it caused me to veer and over steer.
That's why I hit the pier, on the cliff so sheer,
while in first gear.

That strange deer, acting so queer,
seemed to smile and leer,
as I passed so near.

I think that deer enjoyed my fear
and has made a career out of causing such fear;
forcing cars to veer, and sail into the atmosphere
over cliffs so sheer.

As an engineer, I vow to volunteer,
and find that deer.
I'll search far and near;
I'll persevere over the whole frontier.

This deer has a friend who may be a steer.
Together they'll appear, give a cheer, then disappear,
to drink root beer, laugh and sneer.
They're very sincere in their plot of fear and smear.

Bend an ear if you over hear any news of this deer and steer.
I will commandeer both steer and deer.
I promise to end their career of fear
this very year, let me make it clear!

Cora

Cora the cow wouldn't chew her cud,
     she'd much rather chew a tobacco plug.
"This cud tastes quite terrible,
     like cold oatmeal, unbearable."

Cora the cow
     wouldn't go where she was told,
like out of the barn,
     when the mornings were cold.

No, Cora the cow wouldn't go
     where she should be,
she was ornery and stubborn
     as often as she could be.

Cora the cow
     liked to stomp in the mud,
so the farmer had to wash her
     with lots of hot suds.

Cora ate more
     than her share of the feed,
squeezing others out,
     eating more than she'd need.

Cora liked to butt folks
     with her head,
she thought she was a bull (I guess)
     and often saw red.

The rest of Cora's story
     will not be told.
The farmer took her away,
     and then she was sold.

A Story of Survival

Sidney McHale, a prominent male snail,
was caught by a windy gust of a gale,
while on a trail in a lovely vale.
He sailed over a rail landing into a pail,
Someone had left on the trail.

Sidney tried to get out of that pail
but to no avail,
his efforts did fail.
He felt as if he might be in jail.

At the bottom of the pail
was a small bit of khale and
even some light amber ale.

After he ate the khale and drank the ale
he began to wail at the gale that had
caused him to sail and land him into the pail.

While residing in the pail
he noticed a flock of quail walking the trail,
through the lovely vale,
and also a dog wagging his tail.

He needed to hail someone passing this pail
on the trail;
then he would regale them with the tale
Of how he had landed in the pail.

Just about then, a girl pale and frail
(carrying a pail) came along the trail

She saw the pail that held the snail.
She needed another pail
But not a snail.

Tossing the snail out of the pail,
Sydney McHale did sail
over the very same rail,
narrowly missing a nail but
landing safely in the lovely vale.

Two Authors

Glen always carries a pencil and pen;
no matter where, no matter when.

He sleeps in the den,
with Jen,
his pet hen.

Glen's brother Ben
has a pet wren,
named Gwen.

They write stories in their den.
Glen wrote about ten.

Ben wrote one that he never could end.
Glen tried to help Ben again and again.

Ben was his brother and his best friend.
The last I heard they were still in the den,
trying to find a way for Ben's story to end.

If you know how this story should end,
be a friend,
and send your end
to Ben.

Nine Potato Bugs

Nine potato bugs
    all sitting in a group,
were eating there lunch;
    not sandwiches or soup.

Their favorite thing on which to dine,
    were the tender new leaves
on my petunia vine.

"Out of my flower bed!
    Scat and be gone!
You're eating my flowers
    and that is all wrong."

I hit them with the broom
    and sprayed them with the spray.
I smashed all my flowers
    but the bugs got away.

"I hate you bugs,
    I'll get you someday."
But they curled into balls
    and all rolled away.

Bird Uncles

Uncle Ben Gleck lives on a deck;
he has a long neck
and his feathers are flecked.
He notes the deck is just a wreck
as he writes out his monthly rent check.

Uncle Sol Spock lives on a dock.
He's kind of a jock.
He wears a small clock
during his watch on the dock.
He walks and talks and watches out for the hawk.

Uncle Billy Blake lives by a lake.
The best place for Blake
as he is a duck, known as a Drake.
Blake is kind of a flake;
says his feet always ache
to warn of a quake.

Uncle Joe is quite an old crow
who moves ooooooooh
so very, very slow.
But what Joe doesn't know,
isn't worth telling or even to show.

Uncle Hugh Howell is a white snowy owl,
a favorite of all the species of fowl.
His speech is a howl
with an occasional growl,
but never, no never uses a vowel.

Uncle Hank Hawk
Was kind of a jock.
Lots of muscle, not much talk.
Uncle Hank was chief of his flock
With no complaints, not even a squawk.

Pearl

A girl squirrel
By the name of Pearl,
Loved to sing and dance
And sometimes twirl.

Like a bump on a log
Her brother Bob,
Hardly moving at all;
Wouldn't dance or jog.

Bob would rather
Just lay around,
Soaking up sun,
Stretched out on the ground.

If a nut should fall
While Bob was on a limb,
He'd ask Pearl
To go and get it for him.

Squirrels like to chatter
Sing songs or just hum.
Bob was so lazy
He wouldn't chew gum.

Squirrels like to play tag
Leap, jump and run.
Bob thought all games
Were just plain dumb.

Squirrels invited Bob
To come and play games.
He always said, "NO!
But thanks just the same."x

And then one day,
Oh so fateful a day,
A nut fell from a tree
Not too far away.

Bob nodded his head
Towards that nut,
And proceeded to say,
"You know what,"

"Pearl, I see that
you are free,
Will you go get
That nut for me?"

That was Bob's
Great mistake.
The final straw
That took the cake.

Pearl was angry,
Her fur turned red.
If looks could kill
Bob would be dead!

Like the sound of a trumpet,
Very loud, very clear,
Pearl's voice rang out
Causing Bob some fear.

Even the trees shook,
And their limbs trembled,
Rocks rolled around,
The squirrels assembled.

"GET IT YOURSELF BOB!"
Pearl's message so clear,
Other squirrels danced
And gave Pearl a cheer.

And what about Bob?
That furry slob,
He moved away
And got a job.

Fitzhugh Fitzsimmons

Fitzhugh Fitzsimmons was a lengthy worm
Who lived at the corner of Thornberry and Sturm.

All of his friends were spiders and bugs,
Even a few of those slippery green slugs.

Fitzhugh himself was a real fine type,
Gentle, easy going, smoked a briarwood pipe.

His work, his job, or better his trade
(for which I might add was very poorly paid)

Was dangerous, risky, yes risky at best
(he didn't even wear a life saving vest)

But hired himself out as a lure, even bait
To dedicated fisherman who don't mind a long wait.

"Nerves of steel," they said, as he slid down the line,
For minutes, yeah hours in the dark salty brine.

Other worms with less stamina might well fall asleep
As they wait for a fish down so low, so low, in the deep.

Fitzhugh Fitzsimmons was sharp, he was quick
He shimmied up the line when the fish took a nip.

Fitzy, a nickname, just his friends called him that,
Retired from the docks and was given a plaque.

Inscribed on the plaque in brassy letters bold
You could read the moral of this story told.

"This worm so hardworking, so deep in the brine,
Knew just when to shimmey from the nip in time."

My Ma

A big brown bear
    who happened to be my ma,
raised two bear cubs
    without the help of our pa.

Ma was tough,
    ma was stern,
one swipe of her paw
    and my hind-end would burn.

When ma got mad
    she sent us up an old pine tree;
and we didn't come down
    until *she* was ready, no siree!

Sure it was usually danger
    that caused her to scold,
we didn't figure that out,
    we had to be told.

Ma could be tender,
    she had that side when
we cuddled up with her
    in our warm cozy den.

If I'd been boss
    and had my way,
we'd have stayed with ma,
    she'd have never gone away.

My brother,
    he felt that way too;
but there wasn't much
    that we could do.

Yet she had told us
    that it was better that way.
We'd grown pretty big
    and needed to make our own way.

As I look back
    on that sad old day,
I remember a tear fell,
    then she chased us away.

In my heart
    I always sort of blamed pa,
for her running away
        from us and all.

What If

A tiny bug
        about so big by so big
lived under a leaf
        at the end of a twig.

He never traveled far
        from his leafy home.
Even with his many legs
        he still would not roam.

Quite content
        with food found close by,
he'd drink dew off the leaves
        before the sun was high.

Cousins of this bug
        often came to call,
they'd say, "Pal,
        you need to get away from it all."

"Come with us
        to see the sights.
Just a few yards from here
        are the bright lights."

A few yards he mused,
        seemed very far,
I'd might as well consider
        a rocket to a star.

"You'll go to your grave
        never finding what life's about.
Come on," they urged,
        "Pack your bags, and move out."

"But I'm afraid
        of what I'll find out there.
What if I'm different
        and others will stare?

What if they're all smarter
        and think I am dumb?
What if I'm teased
        and they all poke fun?

What if there's danger,
      could I find a place to hide?
What if I get kidnapped
      and taken for a ride?

OR

What if I never
      make a new friend?
What if I never
      see beyond the next bend?

What if I never have to use
      my wits,
do a brave deed
      or read a map on a trip?

What if I never
      discover my talents true?
What if I stay afraid
      my whole life through?

AND

What am I doing
      to help anyone else?
Am I being selfish
      by not sharing myself?

But it's all so scary.
      I've been this way so long.
Could I possibly change,
      could I have been all wrong?

What if I venture too far
      and run into strife?
What if I discover love,
      someone to share my life?

If safety is all
      that a bug desires,
and he just stays home
      by his nice warm fire;

he'd always be afraid,
      he'd always keep his fears.
If I were not just a bug
      I'd shed a few tears."

Don't Scream at a Hummingbird

Don't scream at a Hummingbird, talk in low tones.
Don't yell at a Robin, call him on the phone.

Never but never holler at a Crow,
approach him softly, moving slow.

Creep up carefully, inch by inch,
when you're approaching the Purple Finch.

A telegram maybe the only way
you'll ever get a message to a Blue Jay.

Screech owls may schreech and make lots of noise,
especially at parties they have with the boys.

If you'd like to tell an owl a thing or three,
you'd best send a letter up the old fir tree.

Disciplining Your Spiders

You spiders are putting your webs in all the wrong places!
We're getting you and your webs all over our faces!

You're building them in doorways just about head high.
I'm picking you and your webs from my clothes, hair and eye.

You've built a web from the door to my car.
This just has to stop, you've gone way too far.

Three webs in a cluster I didn't see till too late;
and I was all dressed up, going out on a date.

Go out on a limb or up in a tree;
I won't bother you; you won't bother me.

I don't begrudge a spider his web, just ask that you
build them elsewhere, like my neighbor's instead.

A Rhino Named Rhonda

A rhino named Rhonda
    had a friend who was a clam.
Rhonda loved the seashore,
    that's how the friendship began.

This clam could tell
    a real good joke,
so Rhonda listened carefully
    whenever he spoke.

Friend clam had stories
    about the tide and sea,
and he knew a famous gooey-duck
    who'd been on T.V.

Rhonda told adventure tales
    about the brave and the strong;
the clam listened carefully
    on days that were sunny and long.

What does a rhino
    have in common with a clam?
Not much really
    it's really hard to understand.

And That is That

I see a bat from where I'm at,
What kind of bat am I looking at?

A rat and a cat see that bat
just from where they're sitting at.
Now the cat sees the rat
from where he's at.
Then the rat sees the cat
from where he sat.

I see the bat, the cat, and the rat
from where I am sitting at.
The cat (whose name is Pat)
is really, really, truly fat.
Does the bat know about the cat?
Does the bat know about the rat?

The bat is after a gnat,
He doesn't care about the cat.
The bat caught the gnat,
he doesn't care about the rat.
The rat's no longer where he was at.
The cat's no longer where he had sat.

Alone I sat upon a mat;
I saw a bat, a cat and a rat.
That's all there is, and that is that!

Moth Mothers

Moths have mothers who flutter around,
they fuss and they clean and like to shop downtown.

Moth mothers warn their children to stay close to home;
"The bug zappers could get you if too far you roam."

They lecture their kids about how to take flight;
"And for goodness sake don't get too close to the light!"

Moth mothers have their good points, and they have their bad;
they're opinionated, dogmatic, sometimes rude, sometimes mad.

Moth mothers are jealous of their butterfly cousins;
they gossip over coffee as they gather by the dozens.

Moth mothers are ugly, they have no sense of style;
but that's okay, they only live a very short little while.

A Turtle Named Myrtle

A turtle named Myrtle had low self-esteem;
so she hid in a log, out on a stream.

Even Myrtle the turtle herself had a dream;
the thoughts of it caused her face just to gleam.

Myrtle's dream at first might seem too extreme;
for a turtle who lives in a log on a stream.

Myrtle wanted to sing opera, this was her dream.
A turtle that sings opera?
A turtle with low self-esteem?

This would require a drastic-type scheme.
Myrtle started singing, she tried hard it did seem,
but most of the folks thought they heard Myrtle scream.

The frogs and the turtles that lived on the stream
all got together and they all formed a team.

The team all declared we must form a regime;
Myrtle's singing must stop, it's clearly obscene.

They knew Myrtle suffered from low self-esteem,
so they all brought her presents and lots of ice cream.

And Myrtle stopped singing and she joined the team;
and soon had recovered from her low self-esteem.

The Goldfish

Once there was a young goldfish
who lived in a shallow pie dish,
(his poor tail could barely go swish.)

Well I must say
that's no way for a fish to play,
(or spend a night or a very long day.)

A small boy named Tad
saw the problem he had,
(and felt for the fish, deep down very sad.)

He looked all around
to see what could be found,
(up very high and low very down.)

Just any bowl wouldn't do,
he needed one the fish could see through,
(they could play games like peek-a-boo.)

Cereal bowls? They were out,
not big enough to swim about,
(Tad knew he needed help to work this out.)

Although she moved slow
grandmother would know,
(into which bowl the fish should go).

"A goldfish bowl I haven't got,"
grandmother said, as she thought a deep thought,
(and her fingers played with an old cooking pot.)

"Aha! I've go it! The answer I've found,
just the home for a fish to swim all around,
(swim up very high and dive low very down.)

The answer she had, I knew without a doubt.
From back in the closet grandma brought out,
(an old glass pitcher with a very long spout.)

His Name Was Tex

His name was Tex
And he loved to text
While eating his morning
bowl of chex.

Then his muscles he'd flex
To show off to his dog Rex.
This would vex
Poor Rex.

Tex loved to text those
Of the opposite sex.
They liked to see
His muscles flex.

Unfortunately, those of the opposite sex
Became perplexed as Tex
Put on his thick lens specs.
They also noticed,
His yard filled with wrecks.

Tex was perplexed that
Those of the opposite sex
Were put off by his yard full of wrecks.
But not his dog Rex;
Who liked to see Tex vexed.

Lorn

Early one morn a boy was born,
and they named him Lorn.

His parents had sworn,
his hair would never be shorn.
They looked with scorn
on a head that was shorn.

But why does Lorn
look so forlorn?
Is it because his toe has a corn?
A corn the size of a large acorn.

Lorn had sworn to ignore his corn;
until it broke through the shoe he had worn,
and his new sock that was torn,
by that ugly toe corn.

Lorn looks with scorn at his ugly toe corn;
and he blames it all, on his love of popcorn.

Mona Sue Gravely

Mona Sue Gravely blew bubbles like a pro.
She blew them fast, she blew them slow.
She blew them long, wide and a figure eight,
Round, square, early and late.
She blew bubbles inside bubbles for kids to see.
She blew bubbles that were doubles for adults like me.
Yes Mona Sue was as good as they come
At the challenge of blowing bubble gum.
The end of this tale will make you blue,
It's oh so sad but oh so true.
A thirty inch bubble burst over her face
And the mess it caused brought Mona disgrace.
We started picking gum from her face, hair and neck.
That was three years ago and we're still at it yet!

The Neighbor's Dog

The neighbor's dog has much to say.
It starts in the morning and continues all day.
At night he reminds us of what he has said,
So we'll keep it in mind as we climb into bed.
He always speaks to folks passing by.
It's his mission in life to say it or die.
Lately he's enlisted a short-haired friend.
A young recruit who lives round the bend.
About his mission he is so intense;
Although his desk's behind a six foot fence.

The Police Report

Tall Paul had real gall as he limped into my hall,
stumbled into a wall, took a terrible fall,
and that's what I saw.
The police I did call because of his fall,
and the awl, I found in his paw.
Clearly, Paul had been in a brawl,
outside of the mall.
Due to shock from the fall, I covered Tall Paul
with my granny's wool shawl.
Weak from his fall, Paul struggled to crawl,
in order to scrawl a name on the wall,
using only his claw.
That's all I recall about what happened to Paul,
as I've told chief McCall and the rest of you all.
Signed,
Bugsy Svenhall

Hugh

A kangaroo named Hugh
was home sick with the flu.

He had a brother named Lou
and a sister named Sue.

They had Hugh's flu too.

Hugh's flu made him achy, it's all too true.
Lou's flu and Sue's flu made them sad and blue.

Having the flu is nothing new.
But, having the flu when you're a kangaroo
happens only to a very few.

Hugh, Lou and Sue's flu stuck like glue.

What would you do
if you were a kangaroo
like Hugh with the flu?

You'd go see Dr. Drew McGrue
who works at the zoo.

Sadly, Dr. McGrue told Hugh
he'd just have to weather it through.

Billy Bevelbend

Billy Bevelbend was losing his friends;
he didn't know how, he never knew when.

Billy was smart, he had a good brain,
but sharing with others he thought was a pain.

"I want what's mine! I want what's yours!
Hey come on back—don't go out the door."

Billy would scream, "That kid is a louse,
doesn't he know I'm boss in my house."

"You're a poor sport," Billy would say,
"I don't know why you won't stay and play."

Billy had games, racing cars and walkie-talkies,
basketball, frisbee and electric ice-hockey.

But those games are better when there are two,
just me and myself are really too few.

How was Billy going to get his friends back?
Friends like Horace and Blanche, Ethyl and Mack.

He'd been selfish with them too many times.
They were tired of hearing, "What's mine is mine."

Billy felt ashamed, sorry and a little silly.
What would you do if you were Billy?

An Amphibian's Dilemma

Mable was able to sit at the table,
but preferred to dine on the floor.

Mable was able to sleep in the stable,
but all the horses loudly did snore.

Mable was able to read fiction or fable,
but thought poetry was a terrible bore.

Mable was able to watch T.V. on cable,
but the news scared her, right down to her core.

Sadly, Mable though mostly able, was UNable
to decide whether to live on the lake or the shore.

Emmett

My aunt owned a parrot
    by the name of Emmett.
His favorite phrase was,
    "She didn't buy it, she just rent it."
And he said it like he really mean't it.
    Did Emmett know
what he was saying?
    Or was it a game
that he was playing?

When company came
    to pay a call,
she'd use her silver tea service,
    china cups and all.
And just when the company
    would ooh and ah—aah,
that's when old Emmett
    came on with his call,
"She didn't buy it, she just rent it."
    And he said it like he really meant it.
How embarrassing,
    my aunt would blush,
"It isn't true!" she'd say,
    "Now Emmett you hush!"

If Emmett were mine,
    I'd make him into stew;
and feed him to the vultures
    who live at the zoo.
But auntie would always
    'forgive and forget;'
she'd say,
    "Emmett really is a very nice pet."

But one day auntie
    bought a new car,
A Mercedez diesel,
    her proudest purchase by far.
Of course we had to
    take it for a spin,
up main street, on the freeway
    and around Lake Gwinn.
But oh alas,
    a mistake my aunt made,
she brought that old Emmett
    along in his cage.
It would've been fine
    if a gag she had brought,

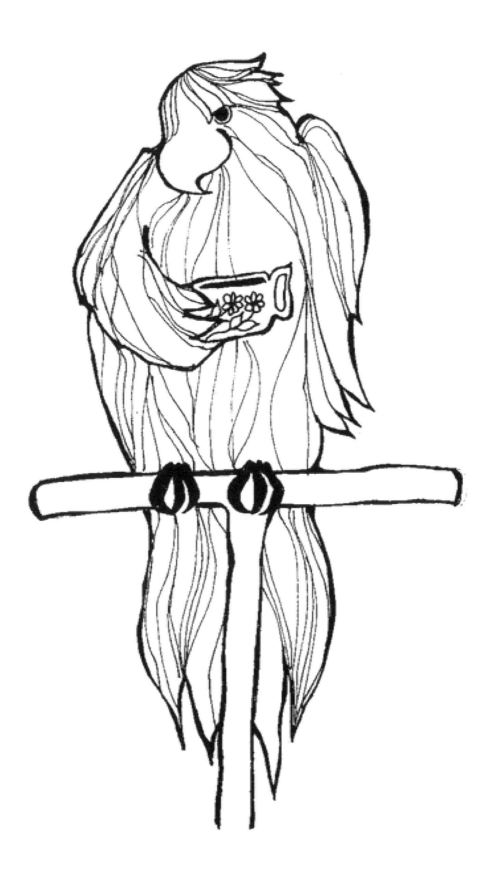

to stifle that bird
    from his sarcastic thought.
We drove up to friends
    and relatives too.
A showing off time,
    a little bragging to do.
We stopped by Fred
    and Laura Sandpiles,
to collect some compliments
    and share a few smiles.
"Where did you buy it?"
    Fred asked with a grin;
and that's when Emmett
    decided to step in.
"She didn't buy it, she just rent it."
    And he said it like he really mean't it.

Back in the car
    I put a bag over his cage;
that old bird was driving me
    into a pink-purple rage.
I gave him a stern warning
    in a few chosen words,
but auntie was soft
    and forgave that old bird.

The next stop was
    the home of Lily LeSnee.
She invited us in
    for crackers and tea.
Your new car is smashing
    friend Lily had said,
it's economical to drive
    and your favorite shade of red.
Then from the cage
    a voice muffled with crackers,
(that old bird
    had really gone whackers)
"She didn't buy it, she just rent it."
    And he said it like he really mean't it.

Then up from her chair
    my aunt arose,
there was something about it,
    my position I froze.
She grabbed that old Emmett
    around his neck,
and walking to the window said,
    "I'm done with forgiving, I'll never forget."

Emmett choked,
  Emmett gasped,
before his eyes
  his whole life shot past.

"What about doing to others
  and the golden rule?
Don't be hasty,
  don't lose your cool!"

Wouldn't you know it,
  my aunt would soften;
she forgave that old bird;
  I'd have bought him a coffin.

Dwight

It was a terrible sight
  as Dwight took flight.

What started as delight
  turned into pure fright
    and a white
      knuckled plight,
        as Dwight,
          who wasn't light
            lost height.

Let's not fight
  or be impolite
    but Dwight
      was not too bright.

Dwight should've tried his flight
  at night
    to have been out of sight.

Dwight wasn't quite right,
  should've stuck with his kite.

As I write,
  I see the blight
    on the landscape left by Dwight.

Birds of Prey

Birds of prey
Dressed in gray,
Sailing over a bay
Longing for May
And a warm sunny day
With a bit of the sun's ray;
Sees a French fry on a tray,
Shouts hurrah and hurray,
It's a very good day,
A day to fly around and play.

Curtis McGrath

A handsome baritone
who happened to be a giraffe,
was known by the stage name
of Curtis McGrath.

His voice was smooth,
his voice was mellow,
his wardrobe stunning
in shades of tan and yellow.

Rhinestone studded scarves
about fourteen yards long;
top hats and tails
and dreamy love songs.

The ladies in the audience
wildly clap and applaud.
Curtis smiles broadly
and bows low for the mob.

Who discovered him,
who made him a star?
Where was he born,
how did he get this far?

His fans were asking
they wanted to know,
and Hollywood wanted him
for another T.V. show.

Curtis was generally silent
about his past;
he preferred not talking,
he preferred you didn't ask.

One day a little girl
approached the giraffe,
she held out a paper
and asked for his autograph.

"Please Mr. Curtis,
would you tell me
how you became so famous,
how it all came to be?"

"I was born in Africa,
out on the plains."
Curtis looked sad
as he began to explain.

"When I was young
(only about eight feet tall)
Mother was taken from me,
I can't remember it all."

"But I remember crying
and being sad and alone,
I needed a friend
and wanted a home."

"I wandered for days
sleeping little at night;
when down flew a tiny bird
who'd been watching my plight.

"You know," he tweeted, "you'd feel
better if you'd hum a little song.
A song makes you feel less lonely
when life's gone all wrong."

"Giraffes barely make noise,
we certainly can't sing.
You'll have to do better,
what other ideas did you bring?"

"Who said you can't sing?
Why don't you try?
I'll bet until now
you didn't know a giraffe could cry."

"That's true," so
while clearing my throat,
"Maybe the bird's right and
I could sing a few notes."

But the sound I heard was
more like a cough or a sputter;
as hard as I tried
that's all I could mutter.

"Keep on trying,"
the tiny bird said,
"I'll keep on helping
while I rest on your head."

Well I did keep trying
(there was nothing else to do)
but it wasn't easy,
just funny sounds came through.

From way down low,
deep in my neck,
gurgles and sputters
were the only sound effects.

And if that wasn't bad enough,
what made it worse,
crowds of animals were gathering
as tiny bird and I rehearsed.

They laughed out loud,
they really jeered.
"I'm going to give up,
It's just as I feared."

Tiny bird kept at it,
 urging me on and on;
"Never mind them, keep on trying
and concentrate on a song."

It's hard when others
come and poke fun.
I wanted to quit,
I wanted to run.

But deep down
way, way down deep,
I knew little bird was right,
I couldn't give into defeat.

Well just as sure
as the sun will rise,
one bright morning
much to my surprise;

a note came forth,
then came two!
They weren't a tune yet
but they were tone true.

I sang a few scales
just to see,
was I only dreaming,
could I stay on key?

I could! I did!
I wanted to do more;
hymns, ballads, anthems
and Broadway show scores.

My animal friends slowly
gathered around,
some looked a little ashamed
and stared at the ground.

But after singing a few
show-stopping tunes,
they clapped, whistled and stomped
and kept me singing till noon.

The animals talked
and spread the news;
soon I was singing to everyone
from chimps to gnus.

The next step was a contract
with a band across the sea.
Tiny bird was my manager,
of course he came with me.

Next were records
and specials for T.V.
Fame came swiftly then
the rest is history.

The really important part
of my story I've shared,
is how Tiny Bird came to me;
how he really cared.

And just because something
might not have been done,
there's always a first time,
don't give up and run.

And don't be surprised
if what you do,
doesn't do some changing
in your friends lives too.

Sydney Slickensides

Sydney Slickenside's home
      is in a hole behind a rock.
This doesn't bother him at all,
      he really likes it a lot.

His favorite thing for doing
      is picking a perfect spot,
then curling up or stretching out,
      when the sun is nice and hot.

He can soak up that sun
      for hours on end,
comfortable and content
      to relax all his bends.

Sydney's needs are simple,
      his food is easily had.
He eats all the good tasting bugs,
      and spits out all of the bad.

If you'd like to visit Sydney,
      I'll tell you a secret I think,
Sydney is very, very shy,
      and moves as fast as a wink.

But if you're careful
      you just might spy,
Sydney soaking up sun,
      watching clouds roll by.

Sydney's a real nice guy you know.
      Don't try to scare him awake;
Sydney's a friend to your garden,
      just a harmless old garter snake.

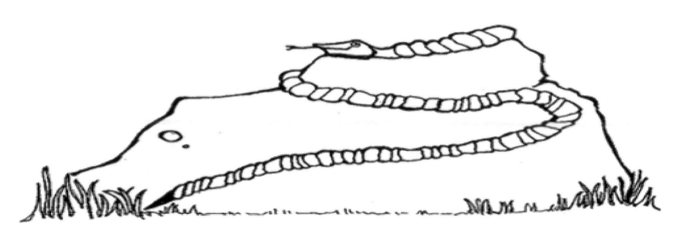

Hilary

Edward Elephant was sad and full of woe,
he'd had a slight accident involving his toe.

He tripped! He stumbled, he landed with a crunch,
right on top of his picnic lunch.

Hilary Hyena had watched the whole scene
and laughed out loud, she could be sorta mean.

To see Hilary laugh made Edward sad, poor dear,
so sad in fact he fought back a tear.

Hilary didn't care, she just moved along,
smiling and whistling and humming a song.

The next thing she saw before her own eyes,
was Penelope Panda baking bamboo pies.

When suddenly, so suddenly without any warning,
a flock of birds took off, as they do in the morning.

Poor Penelope was caught in the rush
and there went her pies, landing like mush.

Hilary had never seen anything so funny;
she laughed so hard she held her tummy.

And did she offer to help Penelope pick up one pie?
If I said she did, I'd be telling a lie.

No, she didn't help, she walked right along,
whistling then humming her same old song.

Before Hilary had gone on, too far,
something sped by her, like a shooting star.

What was it that went by Hilary so fast?
It was Melvin Monkey who'd shot by like a blast.

Melvin had grabbed a branch that was all bent down,
when suddenly it snapped from its snare on the ground.

It happened so fast that Melvin lost hold
and flew through the air, as if a rocket he rode.

First Hilary was startled, but when Melvin crashed in a pile
she started to laugh, and I don't mean just smile.

She grabbed her sides and covered her mouth,
she rolled on the ground, first north then south.

Melvin got up and dusted himself off,
"It wasn't that funny," he said with a cough.

But Hilary moved on, she'd heard a sound nearby,
a muffled moan and then a deep sigh.

In a clearing over by a stream
sat Harrison Hippo and His sister Kathleen.

They had been bathing and were scrubbed real clean,
when high in the treetops (where they couldn't be seen)

some very large birds (don't know what type)
started throwing the fruit that had gotten too ripe.

You guessed it, the hippos had picked the wrong places,
for they both were splattered, even their faces.

Hilary was having a real good day.
Funny things were happening every which way.

She giggled, she laughed, she roared with loud haws,
she ran in circles and clapped her paws.

She laughed so hard she'd shut her eyes
and stumbled right into a honeybee hive.

Yes, Hilary had goofed like all of us do,
and she was off and running in a hurry too.

Hilary was followed by fifty thousand bees,
and do I hear giggling from behind the trees?

Wendell

Aunt Phoebe had a dog
     whose name was Wendell.
He loved dressing up
     in knee socks and sandals.

Some folks make coats for their dogs
     it's true,
for days when the wind blows
     and the snow turns you blue.

I've even seen booties
     on a Chihuahua's feet,
a matching hat and scarf,
     that could look quite neat.

But Wendell dressed up
     on his own in the fall,
plaid pants, V-necked sweaters
     and a matching carry-all.

Or to see him in the spring
     was really something,
shorts and matching tank-top
     the color of pumpkin.

Summers were hard for Wendell
     with his fur and all,
he had to dress lighter
     than he did in the fall.

Usually a sunsuit,
     a straw hat for shade,
then relax under a tree
     and sip lemonade.

Why was Wendell so dapper
     and dressed 'fit to kill?'
He wanted to be a movie star
     and live in Beverly Hills.

Wendell had heard that
     'clothes make the man',
well why not for dogs?
     What a thrill for his fans.

Wendell was no dummy,
     'smart as a whip,' that's plain;
but his character was shallow,
     self-centered and vain.

He spent all his time,
     for hours into days,
dressing and posing
     in the mirror he'd gaze.

His goals were high,
     his dreams were lofty.
His character lacking,
     weak, shaky and faulty.

Hollywood or movies,
     and being a star,
without the hard work,
     he won't get very far.

Castles and princes,
     fairies and queens,
poor Wendell will always
     live in his dreams.

Grant

A communist ant by the name of Shu Grant
never would say I won't or I shan't.
No communist ant would ever say I can't.

Grant worked in the picnic harvesting plant;
which was up on a hill at a very steep slant.

All communist ants love to march and to chant;
and their bosses all love to rave and to rant.
About marching, their bosses are most adamant.

One day Grant refused to march, refused to chant.
This really upset the chief commandant,
who (to tell you the truth) was quite arrogant.

But Grant, for an ant could be most gallivant
and he refused to march and would not recant.

Grant now attends the re-education type plant.

Reptiles Have No Conscience

Reptiles don't care what you think of them
    Or if you talk behind their backs.
Reptiles don't care about your interests,
    They'll tell you lies as truth of fact.

Reptiles aren't bothered
    About doing good;
Or if what they've done
    Is what they should.

Reptiles don't care if
    They're nasty and bad,
Or whether their actions
    Have made you sad.

They'll take what's yours,
    They'll take what's mine.
They'll step on others
    Without a look behind.

Reptiles are deceivers, with looks of wisdom
    Masking treachery and smug.
What appears to be affection can turn into
    A death delivering hug.

Reptiles eventually will show you
    Their real form.
I'll guarantee you,
    It won't be cuddly and warm.

Reptiles can be motionless and quiet
    For quite a little time.
But when crocodiles shed those tears,
    It's for their loss, not yours or mine.

The Lovely Filly

A lovely filly named Millie had a brother named Willie.
Millie was known to be rather silly;
   and she had a mane that was frilly.

Her answers to questions were most willy-nilly.

Willie thought Millie sang rather shrilly.
That's because Millie lived where it was hilly and chilly
   causing her voice to be shrilly.

What do you do with a filly that's silly and sings so shrilly?

Willie took Millie to a place that wasn't chilly or hilly.
He gave her a lily and lace called Chantilly
   to cover her mane that was frilly.

And now they both live in the town called Picadilly.

The Bully

There's a bully on our playground
        and he likes to pick on me.
He's in grade six
        and I'm only in grade three.

He always seems to find me
        when no one else is around.
He calls me a name
        then shoves me to the ground.

One day
        (it was such a disgrace),
he pushed me down
        and sat on my face.

He says if I tattle
        I'm going to need stitches,
all the kids will hate me,
        everyone hates snitches.

If I only had
        a big brother or two.
Boy! Could they pound him,
        what they could do.

I'd like to scare him
        and petrify him like a log.
I could too, I betcha,
        if I had a big dog.

Oh no! I see that bully
        he's coming now.
Should I run or hide,
        fight or . . . wow!

Look who's coming
        just as I talk,
I can't believe it,
        it's my very own pop.

How did Dad know
        that I was so worried?
God heard my prayers
        and He really hurried.

This poem is based on the true story of my little brother.

Maude's Bubblegum Wad

The kid next door whose name is Maude,
is ten years old and has a big yellow dog.

The kid next door whose name is Maude,
is very nice but a little odd.

The kid next door whose name is Maude,
blows pinkish bubbles from a one pound wad.

In her mouth is so much gum,
filling her cheeks and around her tongue;
that her eyes are bulging and her nose is red,
her cheeks too large to go with her head.

It's hard to talk to Maude next door;
her words are jumbled and her diction poor.

I asked her once how she got such a wad.
She answered, *"Ama flu moe smoffle bla pod."*

I couldn't understand her so decided to sneak
a look at how she got all that gum in her cheek.

The answer was simple, each day about four,
Maude bought one stick of gum at the neighborhood store;
and added the new each day to the old
till even Maude's mouth had too much to hold.

Maude finally reached the day, the hour
her face so stretched had lost its power.

She was helpless and pitiful, dazed and glum.
Maude couldn't spit out that wad of gum.

Grandpa Says

Grandpa says:
>When I was young and went to school,
>I'd walk thirty miles a day — as a general rule.

>>Times were hard,
>>Times were tough,
>We didn't turn out any powder puffs.

Grandpa says:
>When I was a boy, I had to chop wood
Enough for all winter and more if I could.

>>Times were hard,
>>Times were tough,
>We didn't turn out any powder puffs.

Grandpa says:
>I had to shovel great mounds of snow.
>Worked in the cold till the frost bit my toe.

>>Times were hard,
>>Times were tough,
>We didn't turn out any powder puffs.

Grandpa says:
>My folks were poor, I had few toys.
>Not like the kids today have to enjoy.

>>Times were hard,
>>Times were tough,
>We didn't turn out any powder puffs.

Grandpa says:
>I didn't have a room I could call mine,
>But shared a bed with my brothers nine.

>>Times were hard,
>>Times were tough,
>We didn't turn out any powder puffs.

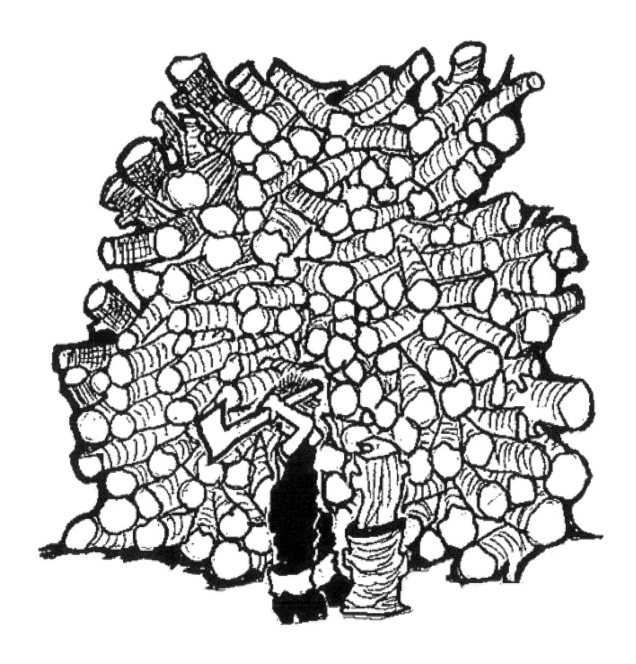

Grandpa says:

    It isn't better to live in times that are hard.
    I can be strong by working in the yard.

    It's good to be a kid, play ball and run,
    You're not a powder puff for having fun.

    The important things in life—it's true—
    Strength is being kind to others different than you.

    Being tough is okay if it means hanging on,
    And not giving up when things go wrong.

Ruel

A mule known as Ruel wanted to quit going to school.
"I'm tired of school!" yelled Ruel, while sitting on a stool.
"Don't be a fool Ruel", said his friends from school.
Ruel thought his friends were cruel,
and started to blubber and pitifully drool.
Ruel's mother said, "Eat your gruel Ruel and go to school."
Ruel's sister Jewel also told Ruel to stay in school.
"I can be cool without school," answered Ruel.
Ruel could be a very stubborn mule.
Ruel quit school and got a job carrying fuel to Liverpool.
Ruel's job isn't cool. Should've stayed in school, Ruel.

Outrage

A large fly flew down from the sky
    AND LANDED ON MY PIE!

He waved hi from his place on my pie.

Leaving my pie he flew onto my tie,
    depositing some of the pie onto my tie;
    before leaving my tie and waving goodbye,
    as he flew back into the sky.

No one wants a fly on their pie or on their tie.

With a sad long sigh I almost started to cry
    when that VERY SAME FLY returned to my pie.

I DO NOT LIE!

Yet not alone did he return to my pie
    but brought three of his friends;
    Ty, Guy and Sheila.

Fooled you, didn't I.

Phyliss and Paul

Two pigeons by the name of Phyliss and Paul
Lived close to a bakery
Next to the mall.

Paul, who was very adept,
Could snatch many crumbs
Before the floor had been swept.

Phyliss, who was keen of sight,
Could catch a morsel
While still in flight.

If you'd ask them, they would tell,
Our life is good,
In fact it's swell.

But then something happened, that's what people said,
The bakery stopped baking
Their cookies and bread.

Very few morsels, hardly a crumb,
What was to happen?
What was to be done?

Together, Phyliss and Paul had done quite well;
Until that time, that troublesome time,
Their economy fell.

"We've got to do something," Phyliss declared,
"We've got to find work
And be better prepared."

Then what happened is really quite rare,
Something floated down,
Floated down through the air.

Was it a French fry or maybe some bread?
The two were hungry,
"They needed to be fed."

Was it some paper or maybe a note?
Could Phyliss read
What someone wrote?

Experience with fortune cookies had taught Phyliss to read.
A skill that for now
Phyliss surely did need.

"Messengers Wanted," is what Phyliss read.
Amazing thoughts then
Entered her head.

The birds knew then just what to do.
With hopeful thoughts
Off they flew.

They're courier pigeons now, Messengers by trade.
Their futures secure,
They have it made.

The Stickleback Brothers

Rodney Stickleback and his brother Ted,
    spent too much money, they were always in the red.
Everything they saw they had to buy,
    candy, games, model cars or kites to fly.
They'd spend all their money and borrow some more.
    "I'll pay you back tomorrow," then slam went the door.
They owed all the family,
    each and everyone.
Mom and dad, grandma and grandpa,
    even a second cousin's uncle's son.
"I've had it with those two," said their dad,
    "they're greedy and grasping,
it's getting real bad.
    They owe everyone in town
and here's what's more,
    I heard they tried to get credit
at the candy store."
    "You're right about that,"
declared their mother,
    "The situation has become
quite a definite bother.
    Let's all get together
and scare them real good.
    They'll stop their spending and borrowing
like they know they should!"
    So all together
the family decided to gather,
    and they brought Sheriff MacFine
to help with the matter.
    "I'm afraid," the sheriff said,
"if you two don't pay what you owe,
    I'll have to put you in jail,
into the hoosegow you'll go.
    You'll have until morning
to pay everyone back
    or your toothbrush and p.j.'s
you'd better get packed."
    Well Rodney and Ted
were filled with tears and woe,
    upon adding it up,
eighty-three-seventy was the sum they did owe.
    "We're in big trouble Rodney,"
cried brother Ted.
    "I don't know about you,
but the thoughts of jail
    fill me with dread."

Rodney wailed,
    "Me too brother Ted,
jails are known
    for their very hard beds.
We haven't got the money,
    we haven't got the dough.
Mom and dad wouldn't really
    send us to jail you know.
Nah! They're just bluffing,"
    Rodney decided to believe.
But in the morning
    in the jail,
the two were received.
    Soon half the town
gathered around,
    and from behind the bars,
the pair listened to their sound.
    "You two must promise
to learn some new habits,
    remember, friends and money
don't multiply like rabbits.
    You've been irresponsible,
you've shown real greed.
    From now on you must learn
to buy just what you need.
    Well not only that,
you'll pay everyone back;
    we're not just chatting,
we're stating the facts."
    Rodney and Ted promised
they would not fail.
    So the other half of town
came up with their bail.
    The Stickleback brothers
learned the hard way,
    too much borrowing and spending
just doesn't pay.
    Now the brothers are happy,
now they're content.
    They borrow from the library
and never spend a cent.

May and June

"I'm so tired of school," said May.

"Well hang on," said June,
"it'll be out any day."

"Oh, is that true, will it be very soon?"

"I can promise you that
or my name isn't June."

Nate and Kate

Nate's legs numbered eight.
Nate was a spider,
 so eight legs were his fate.

Nate lived in a crate
 which he thought was great.
Nate's web in the crate was A-1 first rate.
 It's where he slept and where he ate.

This first rate web was also bait;
 for flies who came in, Nate ate.

Nate's girl friend was Kate.
 She had eight legs just like Nate,
 plus she'd learned how to skate.

Never late for a date,
 Nate served Kate piles of flies
 heaped upon her plate.

Nate's web had a gate
 and all his lines were perfectly straight.
 Straight lines were a trait of Nate's.

Kate was so impressed by Nate
 and Nate by Kate and how she could skate
 that she soon became Nate's mate.

The Convention

There's a convention in my yard,
it's such a noisy affair.
I wish they'd all just leave
and go away from there.

There are debates and speeches,
everyone has their say,
I wish they'd just adjourn,
I wish they'd go away.

Their fervor seems political.
Each delegate is so intense.
And yet they're all united
and few are on the fence.

The gavel must have sounded,
the delegates are leaving my trees.
The next convention will convene
whenever the delegates please.

The Intermission

Watch out little bug,
  look over your shoulder,
you'd better move faster
  if you want to grow older.

Say bird, what's that sneaking up
  behind that tree?
Fly away quickly or
  a cat's lunch you'll be.

Oh hey Mr. cat,
  better forget this chase,
it seems a dog
  has joined the race.

Hear that horse whinney?
  I know the sound.
That horse may try to kick
  that dog out of bounds.

Even a horse
  can have a bad day,
for down from the mountains
  comes a cougar to play.

Up in that tree,
  what's that owl up to?
Looks like he's hungry
  for gray mouse stew.

Here's a great large eagle
  whose hunger won't keep.
Play it safe little fish
  and stay down in the deep.

Over here we see,
  a jackrabbit on the run.
The old gray coyote
  wants more than just fun.

And back to the fish
  who from the eagle escaped,
he's after a minnow
  for his dinner plate.

This is a surprise!
      What a turn around,
all the animals are resting
      in a clearing on the ground.

Let's be quiet and listen,
      to hear what they say,
could this be intermission
      in the chase for today?

"Say, friend dog,
      won't it be a better day
when we'll all be friends
      and won't chase this way?"

"Yes... I guess so,
      I just had a close call.
If that horse improves his aim,
      it's all over, I'm done! And that's all."

"Well, listen dog,
      a horse has his enemies and foes,
that cougar over there has sharp teeth
      and claws in his toes."

"What about me?
      I just try to get along,
just a simple little bug,
      I don't bother anyone."

"Well, I'll tell you this,
      and just a little more,
cats to me are
      certainly a bore."

Just when it's time
      to sit on my nest,
some miserable cat comes,
      to disturb my rest!"

"I'm fast and I'm speedy,
      built to hop and to run,
but it sure would be nice
      just to stretch out
and soak up some sun."

"We coyotes get hungry
      for rabbit the most,
but we have enemies hunting us
      who like coyote pot-roast."

"Well I don't know
        if I want to change,
I like the thrill of the hunt
        on the wide open range.
Maybe because I don't live with your fear.
        Cougars have fewer enemies
to guard from the rear."

"You *don't* do you,
        lest you forget,
the man with the weapon,
        the man with the trap!"

"And often our dread
        is from our own kind,
it's especially sad
        but always in our mind."

"But cat, did you say
        someday things
will be different,
        it won't always be this way?"

"Well the scriptures say,
        God's kingdom will come,
everything's going to be different,
        everything under the sun."

"The lion is supposed to
        lay down with the lamb.
Maybe he'll be eating
        peanut butter and jam."

"Well, I see a lot
        as I soar through the clouds,
the cry of creation
        can be very loud."

"That day can't come too soon
        to satisfy me.
I can say it for everyone,
        from the elephant to the bee."

But intermission is over,
        for now at least,
may *Thy* kingdom come
        for man and beast!"

The Quarrel

"You hit my leg!"
"You took my hat!"
"That's only cuz you used my bat!"

"Just cuz you're older—
      you're such a snob.
Just cuz I'm younger
      you treat me like a blob."

"You're the baby,
      you always pout and cry;
mother's little darling
      is a tattletale and spy!"

"Aw, leave him alone,
      bug someone your own size,
you're so creepy
      all your best friends are flies!"

"How'd you get in this
      you pitiful little bore?
I wouldn't waste time on you
      you're rotten to the core."

"How would you know?
      You're so dumb,
you should live in a swamp
      and drink slimy green scum."

"Hey peanut brain,
      your I.Q.'s no prize.
You have a great future
      sorting worms by their size."

"At least I'll earn money
      when you're in a padded cell.
At least whatever I do,
      I do very well."

"If I'm in a padded cell
      it's because I live with you!
A few more years like this
      we'll all be crazy and batty too."

"Well, you're just a wimp
      and here's what's more,
you've got a bat in your attic and
      you're rowing with one oar!"

"I think you're both flakey,
      you're both real dips;
mom should of sued the stork,
      she really got gypped."

"Hey! The rain stopped,
      I"ll race you to the door."
"Don't forget your mitt
and the ball is on the floor."

The Mole

A mole in a hole,
carrying a bowl,
lived next to a mean, nasty troll
on a cliff ovcrlooking a shoal.
He was taking a poll on
what would be the toll
on leaving his hole,
using a pole
to jump over the shoal.

Two Bunnies

A bunny named Sonny
Was chummy
With a bunny who was funny.

Sonny would laugh
Until his eyes were runny,
At the funny bunny.

The bunny who was funny
Loved eating toast and honey
On days that were sunny.

But the bunny who was funny
Had no money for toast and honey,
And that wasn't funny, that was crummy.

So Sonny hired the funny bunny to be funny
while he sold his candy that was gummy
And together they made lots of money.

Then they both ate toast and honey
On days that were sunny.
Sonny was no dummy of a bunny.

Gerry's Ferry

They called her merry Gerry.
She was the captain of the ferry.
Many years and many cars
did Gerry's ferry carry.

Gerry's husband Harry
ran the family dairy.
Gerry and Harry had a son Larry
and a daughter Mary.

Larry and Mary found the dairy and ferry scary;
so they left our town of McClarry
and moved out on the prairie
where they raise a rare type of cherry.

We need not tarry over the fact
that Larry and Mary
were rather contrary.

The town will miss Gerry
and her little yellow canary
always with her on the ferry.

Gerry was not known to tarry
when running the ferry,
and of the weather she was very wary.

Today we bury Gerry.
Let's raise a glass of sherry
to our beloved Gerry,
The captain of the ferry.

Wayne

Wayne slid down the drain,
  it caused him some pain,
    the drain was meant for rain,
      but he wanted to gain
        quick access to the train
          that was going to Maine.

His actions were inane;
  he didn't use his brain,
    sometimes he's so vain.

Due to that drain
  Wayne now uses a cane
    as he strolls down the lane.

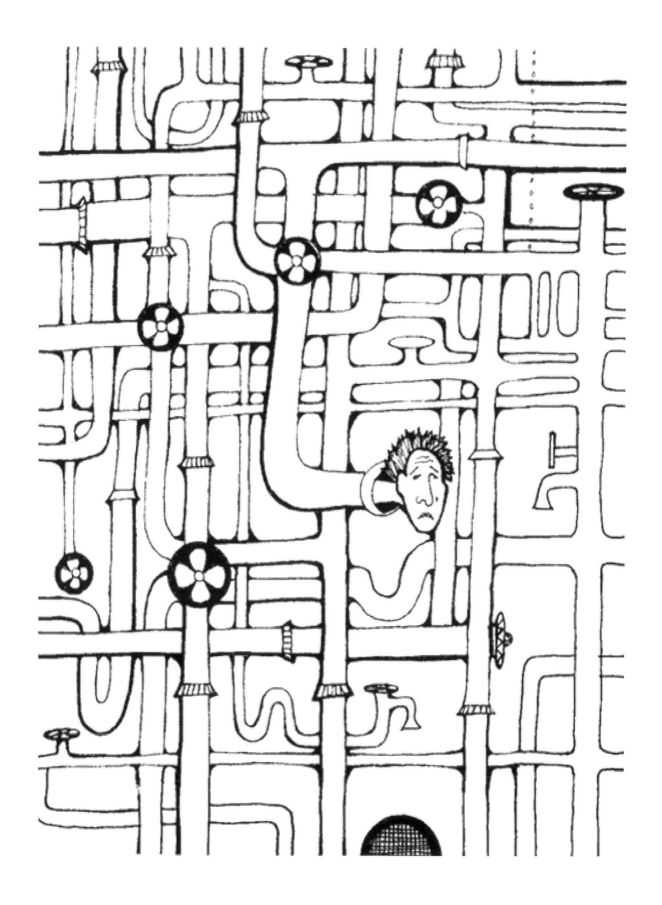

Jake and the Rake

A snake known as Jake slid over a rake,
on his way to some cake,
that had fallen on the ground.

Sliding over the rake on his way to the cake
had been a mistake for his belly got scraped
on the rake and began to ache,
as he very soon found.

Jake slid to a lake just for the sake,
that his belly did ache (from crossing that rake)
beyond a green, grassy mound.

Emerging from the lake he avoided the rake
that had caused his belly to ache
on his way to the cake
that had fallen on the ground.

In order to partake of that very same cake,
he would now undertake
a new path that he'd take
to get hold of that cake,
just over the mound.

Feel sorry for Jake,
when he got to the cake,
took a bite of the cake, he found it a fake,
his fang he did break,
and it made a terrible sound.

Stuart McDingledong

Stuart McDingledong blew one bubble for all time.
It was very large and had a shape that was fine.

Yet Stuart had only a one bubble career,
for something happened that caused him great fear.

This bubble so pink so grand in size
lifted Stuart on up, to float through the skies.

He hopes for now the bubble won't burst,
for then his fate could be the worst.

Stuart and his bubble caught a westerly breeze
that carried him dangerously close to some trees.

A flock of birds flew above Stuart's head,
with beaks that were sharp and claws that could shred.

Passengers waved as their plane flew by.
Stuart could see them out of the corner of his eye.

Although this trip was kind of fun,
Stuart's jaw was tired from holding that gum.

Perhaps he'd meet a skydiving band;
they might share their parachute and bring Stuart to land.

Or maybe a balloonist will just happen by
and snatch Stuart in her basket as she soars through the sky.

For now we'll hope that his bubble stays round
and nothing will happen to make Stuart crash down.

Harvey Hasdroodle

Harvey Hasdroodle was a very proud poodle,
who thought he was better than others.

I'm taller and handsomer than all of my friends,
or certainly my sisters and brothers.

My fur is the curliest with the shiniest sheen.
My character flawless (I've never been mean.)

I can jump in great bounds
or track like blood hounds;

My brain is sharp, I do mean fine.
I'll learn to spell in a matter of time.

I only have one tiny flaw,
I'm not too modest, no, not at all.

The Joke and the Bloke

A nasty bloke played a joke
by throwing eggs upon some folks.

The eggs broke, spilling the yolks,
soaking their cloaks with yellow yolks.

The folks seeing their cloaks
soaked with messy yolks,
spoke to the bloke about his joke;
then proceeded to choke and poke the bloke
until he just about did croak.

The bloke never soaked folks with yolks
on their cloaks or ever again played
such a joke again on folks.

Be careful the folks you joke,
or the yolks and the joke
might be on you—the bloke.

Mildred and Fred

Mildred and Fred had a shed painted red.

Mildred and Fred had an extra long bed.

Mildred and Fred shared a body
  but each had their own head.

Mildred and Fred had a chicken coupe
  but raised rats instead.
Mildred and Fred fed on rat stew
  and white bread.

Mildred and Fred had no reason to get wed.
They were as one, until they were dead.

And that's just what the preacher had said.

Seagulls

Seagulls screech, swoop and scold,
They have long legs and wings that fold.
They don't like geese, ducks or dogs,
They act quite superior from their perch on the logs.
They're not generous when it comes to food,
They're better described as downright rude.
Seagulls love clams and especially French fries.
Get out of their way as they dive from the skies.
Seagulls as friends would not be cool.
They're irritable and crabby as a general rule.
If I see one, I'll just keep walkin,
And pay no attention to his loud-mouth squawkin.

Millicent Wright

Millicent Wright was such a sight
as she rode her bike late at night;
dressed in veils of white,
causing folks a terrible fright.

Millicent's plight?
Her poor eyesight;
and her bike, that had no light.
And yet, she rode at night
in pure unabashed delight.

Millicent's brain must not be right;
she might be sick or not too bright.

Some got mad and wanted to fight.
"We will unite on Millicent's right
to ride her bike so late at night,
with or without a light that's bright".

Millicent Wright's appetite,
for riding at night
was short-lived or some said slight.
On one steep hill her bike took flight,
and gained great height.
With limited sight, (quite an oversight)
Millicent's landing cured her delight
in riding her bike in the dark of night
without a light, in veils of white.

Sibling Rivalry

Pat is a fat brat.
Pat looks like a rat so he wears a big hat.
Pat's brain is the size of a gnat.
Pat hates the cat, named Chat and always carries a bat.
When Pat sat, the chair went flat so he has to sit on a mat.
Why do I hate Pat?
Because Pat IS a rat and he's a brat.
Signed,
Pat's brother Matt
Pat and Matt are having a spat!

Poor Dean

Arlene was the queen of clean.

She married Dean, who became kind of mean,
after marrying Arlene.

Arlene insisted that Dean, stay perfectly clean,
at all times and even between.

She was often seen, scrubbing poor Dean,
while he worked in the yard, to keep it so green,
and she used soap with chlorine.

Dean's been heard to scream a scream,
that could shatter your nerves,
from your toes to your spleen.

Arlene's obsession with clean, was clearly obscene,
and her therapist said,
it started when Arlene was a teen.

Her mother Irene was an absolute fiend
as to Arlene's having to eat
each and every green bean.

Her sister, Kathleen, tried to convene,
a meeting with Arlene,
and intervene on behalf of poor Dean.

The answer was seen to divert Arlene,
so she'd no longer demean her husband,
poor Dean, about staying clean.

Arlene is still pretty clean,
but now has a routine.
She plays tambourine,
in a canteen, in the town of Aberdeen.

This leaves poor Dean,
to be dirty or clean,
and not overseen by his wife Arlene.

He no longer screams or even is mean,
and has given up his craving for nasty nicotine.

Rod and Claude

An odd frog named Rod
wore shoes known as clogs;
unusual for a frog.

He lived in a bog
and often sat on a log;
that wasn't odd for a frog, but....
He had a friend named Claude
who happened to be a dog
and they traveled abroad.
Rod hosted a travelogue from his log
while he blogged and kept a catalogue
of his travels with Claude.
Often the fog was dense in the bog.
That's why Claude and Rod
like to travel abroad.
Rod and Claude together drank grog
and engaged in dialogue
about conditions in the bog.
Rod liked to jog in his clogs
on a track in a quad near to the bog.
Claude formed a squad with another dog
to protect Rod while he jogged in the quad.

A dog named Claude who's friends with a frog
who wears clogs while he jogs
maybe just as odd as a frog named Rod.

Bubblegum Index

Alphabetical Index

In Order of the Book Index

Annette "Aunty Nett" Proctor is a retired art teacher who taught kindergarten through twelfth grade students for twenty-two years. She is highly trained vocalist and graduated from the University of Washington with a Voice Major. She has sung in several operas and was offered a coveted scholarship to train and sing opera in Italy. She is a mother of four now adult children and currently lives in Washington State. She volunteers with her local church and once a month teaches art to the homeless at the Seattle Union Gospel Mission. She enjoys travelling, painting and composing poetry—often in her sleep.

Made in the USA
San Bernardino, CA
20 June 2014